PICK YOUR PATH #1

by Ray Santos
illustrated by Caravan Studio

Grosset & Dunlap
An Imprint of Penguin Group (USA) LLC

GROSSET & DUNLAP
Published by the Penguin Group
Penguin Group (USA) LLC, 375 Hudson Street, New York, New York 10014, USA

USA | Canada | UK | Ireland | Australia | New Zealand | India | South Africa | China

penguin.com
A Penguin Random House Company

Published by Grosset & Dunlap, a division of Penguin Young Readers Group, 345 Hudson Street, New York, New York 10014. GROSSET & DUNLAP is a trademark of Penguin Group (USA) LLC. Printed in the USA.

ISBN 978-0-448-48347-4 10 9 8 7 6 5 4 3 2 1

The final class of the day comes to an end, and Guren Nash can't wait to get out of school. He has plans to meet up with his friends later, but he is looking forward to spending a few quiet hours at home—no schoolwork, no battling evil monsters from another world, no pressure to do anything but play with his cat, Max.

But as always, his dreams of a relaxing afternoon are cut short as his white Tenkai Core Brick begins to glow in his pocket. He knows exactly what that means. Alongside his friends Ceylan Jones, Toxsa Dalton, and Chooki Mason, he is one of the legendary Tenkai Knights. It is their duty to protect the planet of Quarton from the evil Vilius and his relentless minions, the Corrupted. Once the boys are summoned, they have to transport to Quarton via an Interdimensional Portal. It's hidden away in their friend and mentor Mr. White's Shop of Wonders, an old junk shop that never seems to have any customers.

Guren pauses, holding the Tenkai Core Brick in his hand. He can feel that something is seriously wrong on Quarton. If he waits for his friends, it might be too late by the time they get to Quarton. Then again, Mr. White always tells them that the Tenkai Knights are stronger as a team. Maybe Guren should wait for the others before heading to Mr. White's shop—or maybe waiting is a mistake.

If Guren should head to Quarton on his own, head to page 48

If Guren should wait for his friends, head to page 17

Guren can't believe he wasted so much time exploring that strange street. Still, he can't help but think something is up. Leaving the mysterious street behind him, he runs as fast as he can to Mr. White's shop. His friends must have gone to Quarton

without him, and he doesn't like the idea that he's let them down.

As he arrives at Mr. White's, Guren notices that the old man doesn't look happy.

"Guren, what took you so long?" asks Mr. White. "The others have gone to Quarton without you. Beag has been taken by Vilius. They have gone to rescue him."

"I'm sorry, Mr. White," he replies. "Something came up."

"Guren, you know the importance of teamwork," says Mr. White. "You've all learned that lesson many times already."

Guren hangs his head. "I know. I feel really bad. I hope I didn't let down the rest of the team. Or Beag."

Mr. White gives him a comforting smile. "You should get going. I'm sure they could use Bravenwolf's help."

Guren arrives on Quarton after shapeshifting into Bravenwolf. In the distance, he can see his friends, the other Tenkai Knights, battling a group of Sky Griffins. Around them, dozens of Corekai and Corrupted soldiers are also fighting.

As Bravenwolf prepares to join his friends in battle, he spots Granox sneaking off.

If Bravenwolf should follow Granox, head to page 52

If Bravenwolf should join up with the others to fight the Sky Griffins, head to page 54

It is difficult and scary to say no to Wakame, but Guren has a feeling there is some real trouble on Quarton. Maybe if he promises to bring everyone back later to help, she won't be so angry.

If Guren decides to stay and help Wakame, head to page 19

If Guren promises to come back later and help, head to page 80

Bravenwolf makes his way through the darkness. The corridor seems to go on forever. In the distance he sees a flickering light and quickly makes his way toward it. After only a few steps, the floor gives out from under him and he crashes onto hard ground far below.

As he rolls over onto his back, the room lights up. He looks around and finds that he is in a deep dirt pit. Above him, he sees Granox standing at the edge of the pit, surrounded by dozens of Corrupted soldiers.

"Better luck next time!" says Granox with an evil laugh.

The End

"We need to stick together," Guren says, looking to Mr. White for support.

"Yeah, we've always been stronger as a group," Chooki adds as the four boys high-five.

Mr. White nods approvingly as the boys prepare to teleport to Quarton together.

Arriving on the planet as the Tenkai Knights, the boys have shapeshifted into Bravenwolf, Tributon, Lydendor, and Valorn.

"All four Tenkai Knights? We are certainly fortunate," a Corekai soldier announces with joy.

"Any idea where Beag might be?" Bravenwolf asks.

"We think he might be in a Corrupted compound just over that ridge," the soldier replies and points off to the west. "It's being guarded by Shadius. I don't think we can hold our position here if we decide to take him on. We've had word that Vilius and his army are on their way to this location. We really could use the Tenkai Knights to help us fend him off."

"That's no problem," Valorn says. "We're here now. We'll just charge in like I did last night with the zombie goblin castle in *Undead Beast Fighter Six*. We'll be back before old Vilius gets here."

If the Tenkai Knights should battle Shadius and try to rescue Beag before Vilius arrives, **head to page 37**

If the Tenkai Knights should try to fend off Vilius before rescuing Beag, **head to page 67**

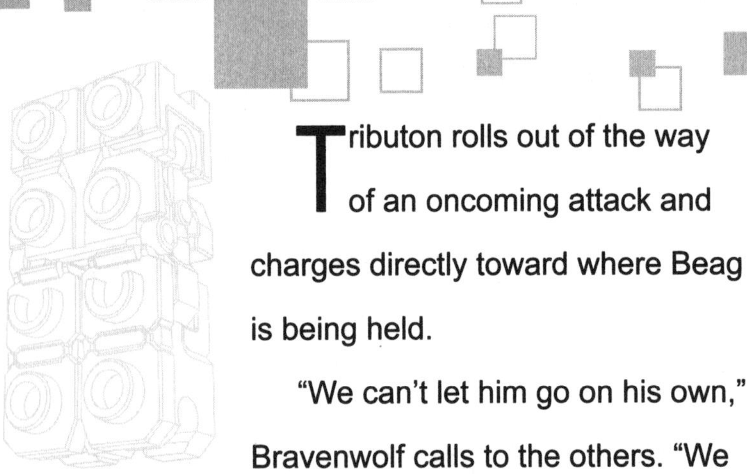

Tributon rolls out of the way of an oncoming attack and charges directly toward where Beag is being held.

"We can't let him go on his own," Bravenwolf calls to the others. "We have to help him."

Slyger waits as Tributon and the other Tenkai Knights approach. Then he holds up one arm. "Corrupted, raise the Energy Nets!" he commands.

The ground beneath the Tenkai Knights shudders as a large glowing net appears below them. They immediately try to tear through it with their weapons and shields, but the powerful Corrupted Energy is too much.

In the distance, they can hear Vilius laughing.

The End

Guren has learned that the Tenkai Knights are much stronger as a team. He knows that he needs to wait for his friends to arrive before heading to Mr. White's shop. It doesn't take long, and the four boys are together on their way to whatever trouble has called them to Quarton.

"Ah, boys, I'm so glad that you are all here," says Mr. White as he rushes them through the shop to the Interdimensional Portal that will send them to Quarton. "There's no time to waste."

"What, no snacks this time?" Toxsa asks. "How am I supposed to fight bad guys on an empty stomach?"

"Give it a break, dude," Ceylan adds. "I saw you eat two lunches today."

"I'm not sure the cafeteria hamburgers count as food," Toxsa says as they step up to the portal.

“Boys, Vilius and the Corrupted army have captured Beag, the commander of the Corekai army,” Mr. White informs them. “You must hurry if you are to rescue him. The Corekai have tracked them to two possible locations. It might be too dangerous to split up, but if you stick together, you’d better move quickly. Beag doesn’t have much time.”

If the Tenkai Knights should split up and explore both locations, head to page 42

If the Tenkai Knights should head to Quarton as a team, head to page 13

"Great!" Wakame says as she drags Guren back to her family's restaurant.

When they arrive, Guren sees a stack of cardboard boxes piled up in the middle of the restaurant.

"Our monthly order of supplies came in this morning," she says. "I need you to move them into the storage room. And make sure you put them all in the right place. I'll check to make sure you did it right."

Forty minutes later, Guren has hauled the last of the boxes into the storage room. He wipes the sweat from his brow and checks his watch. He's spent too much time with Wakame—he needs to get to Mr. White's shop!

"Hmmm," Wakame says as she steps into the room and inspects the boxes. "I guess this will have to do. Now let's talk about all the dirty dishes from the lunch rush. They're not going to wash themselves."

If Guren tells Wakame that he's done enough and needs to leave, head to page 60

If Guren stays to wash dishes, head to page 50

"We need to defeat Vilius," Bravenwolf calls to the others. "That's our only hope to rescue Beag."

"Looks like it's time for Tenkai Titan Mode," Lydendor announces.

TENKAI ENERGY AT 100 PERCENT. ACTIVATING TENKAI TITAN MODE.

At once, the four Tenkai Knights begin shapeshifting into the giant Titan versions of their Tenkai Knight forms.

Vilius laughs as he orders his Corrupted soldiers to attack the Tenkai Knights. "You're not the only ones with that ability."

Just like the Tenkai Knights, Vilius shapeshifts into Titan Mode.

Behind Vilius, Tributon spots Beag being held by a Corrupted soldier called Slyger. "I see Beag," he says to the others. "I'm going to go rescue him."

"No, Tributon," Lydendor calls out. "It's a trap. If we take our focus off Vilius, we'll lose our advantage. Then we wouldn't be able to save Beag . . . or ourselves."

If you think the Tenkai Knights should stay and battle Vilius, head to page 72

If you think the Tenkai Knights should try to rescue Beag, head to page 16

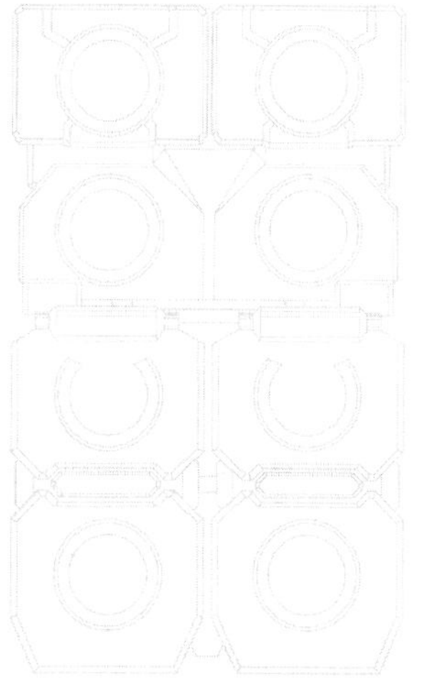

Bravenwolf watches as Tributon charges off on his own toward the War Stallions. Bravenwolf doesn't feel good about letting his friend head off into battle on his own, but he knows that if Vilius tries to ambush them, he'll be ready.

Just as the fight begins, two other figures appear in the distance: Lydendor and Valorn! Bravenwolf is excited to see his friends. But his joy is cut short as a shadow falls over the battlefield.

It's Vilius and an army of his Corrupted soldiers. Bravenwolf was right—it had been a trap all along. Bravenwolf ducks behind a large stone outcropping. Luckily, Vilius hasn't spotted him. At least, not yet.

Vilius chuckles as waves of Corrupted charge toward the three Knights.

Bravenwolf's friends need his help. He has to join them—but he also knows that this could be his chance to defeat Vilius once and for all.

If Bravenwolf should try to ambush Vilius, head to page 44

If Bravenwolf should join his friends and battle the Corrupted army, head to page 56

Titan Vilius rises up into the air and readies his attack. Behind him, the Tenkai Knights see a group of Corrupted soldiers dragging out a weary-looking Beag.

"Look," Tributon calls out. "We need to rescue him."

"Keep your attacks focused on Vilius," says Bravenwolf. "That's the only way we can save Beag. We won't be able to help him until Vilius is defeated."

Bravenwolf readies his special Tenkai Titan attack, the Wolf Cannon.

"He's right," Lydendor says as he raises his weapon, the mighty Chainsaber. "Vilius is our number one target. We have to focus on him."

"What if he's distracting us while his soldiers

head off with Beag?" says Valorn. "This could be our last chance to save our friend."

If Bravenwolf decides to listen to Valorn, head to page 70

If Bravenwolf lets Tributon go and continues with the Wolf Cannon, head to page 77

Bravenwolf and Tributon charge toward the three massive War Stallions that stand guard outside the small bunker where the Corekai believe Beag is being held captive.

"I don't have a good feeling about this," Tributon

says as the giant beasts turn to face them.

"Me neither," Bravenwolf replies. "But we have to rescue Beag. This is our only option."

As the Tenkai Knights close in, the lead stallion rears up and prepares to attack. Tributon raises his bow and blasts a Tenkai Energy Arrow at the beast. Bravenwolf raises his sword and charges right at the enemy.

Tenkai Energy explodes around them as arrow after arrow strikes its target, and sword attacks knock back the War Stallions.

Just then a familiar voice rings through the air.

"Oh man, you can't finish this level without us," says Valorn. "I hate missing out on the action."

Lydendor and Valorn have arrived!

But they aren't alone—behind them scores of Corrupted soldiers scamper over the hill and toward them.

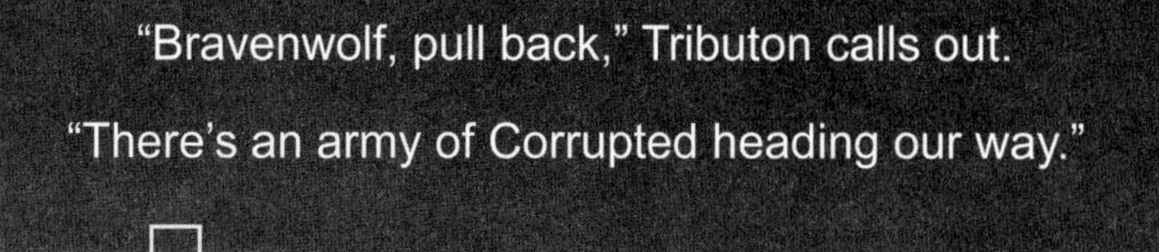

"Bravenwolf, pull back," Tributon calls out. "There's an army of Corrupted heading our way."

If Bravenwolf should pull back and join the others, head to page 56

If Bravenwolf should continue battling the War Stallions, head to page 47

Tributon sprints off in the direction of where Beag is being held. Seconds later he vanishes from sight.

"Where did he go?" Bravenwolf calls to the others while running to find his friend. "We have to find him."

"Hold up," Lydendor yells to Bravenwolf. "I don't like the looks of this."

It's too late. The ground opens up under Bravenwolf, and the Tenkai Knights fall into a dark pit below. He tries to find something to hold on to, but there is nothing but seemingly endless darkness.

The End

Guren decides to explore the strange street. As he turns the corner, he can still sense flickers of Tenkai Energy surging through the city. *Is there something special about this street?* he wonders. Maybe it has something to do with why he's being called to Quarton.

He searches every corner and every alley, but can't find anything.

As he walks farther along, Guren starts to feel less and less that there is something worth searching for down this street. Perhaps something is trying to distract him from heading to Quarton? Guren needs to get to Mr. White's shop. He turns and starts running.

Head to page 6

Bravenwolf knows that Valorn is right. Their mission is to rescue Beag. The fight with Vilius will have to wait until another day.

"Okay, guys," Bravenwolf says. "Rescuing Beag is our number one priority. But I don't think we can sneak in."

"Yeah," Lydendor agrees. "We need to tackle this head-on."

"Tributon," Bravenwolf says. "Keep your fire on Vilius. See if you can hold him off long enough for the rest of us to overtake Slyger. Once we take him down, we can help with Vilius."

"I'll do my best," says Tributon as he volleys more Tenkai Energy bolts at Vilius.

Vilius just laughs at them as he deflects the Energy attacks with his sword.

"I need to stay and help Tributon," Bravenwolf says. "Valorn and Lydendor, it's up to you two to free Beag."

Lydendor charges forward, slashing at the oncoming Corrupted soldiers with his powerful Chainsaber. Behind him, Valorn blasts away with bolts of Energy from his spear.

The Corrupted army begins to flee, but the villain Slyger stands his ground. Behind him, a wounded Beag struggles with his captors.

"Give it up," says Lydendor as the Corrupted soldiers protecting Slyger flee.

"Never," Slyger replies. "You'll never get your friend back."

"I wouldn't be so sure," says a voice from behind the villain.

Slyger spins around to see a freed Beag surrounded by dozens of Corekai soldiers.

Lydendor and Valorn turn their attention back to Vilius. With the four Tenkai Knights and Beag leading the Corekai army, Vilius knows he is defeated.

The End

The four Tenkai Knights cautiously make their way over the ridge and spot Shadius and his Corrupted soldiers guarding a small compound.

"We have to move quickly," Valorn says. "If they spot us, we'll never be able to rescue Beag before Vilius gets to the Corekai."

"I think we need to head back," says Lydendor. "There are way too many. Even if we do beat them, we'll be in no shape to fight Vilius."

If the Tenkai Knights should stay and fight Shadius, head to page 46

If the Tenkai Knights should head back and fight Vilius, head to page 68

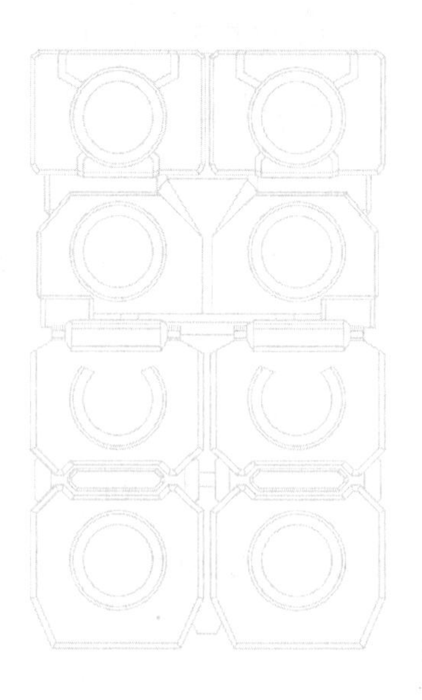

"The only way we're going to defeat these guys is to stick together," says Bravenwolf.

"Well, yeah," adds Valorn. "That and Titan Mode."

"Agreed," say the other three Tenkai Knights.

TENKAI ENERGY AT 100 PERCENT. ACTIVATING TENKAI TITAN MODE.

At once, the four Tenkai Knights begin shapeshifting into the giant Titan versions of their Tenkai Knight forms.

"Ha-ha-ha." A deep voice rumbles behind them. "That might be enough to stop my Corrupted army. But you still need to get through me."

“Vilius!” Lydendor yells.

Behind Vilius, Tributon spots Beag being held by the Corrupted soldier called Slyger. “I see Beag,” he says to the others. “I’m going to go rescue him.”

“No, Tributon,” Lydendor calls out. “It’s a trap. If we take our focus off Vilius, we’ll lose our advantage and we won’t be able to save Beag . . . or ourselves.”

If you think the Tenkai Knights should go after Vilius first, head to page 25

If you think the Tenkai Knights should try to rescue Beag, head to page 16

Guren transports to Quarton and shapeshifts into the Tenkai Knight Bravenwolf. Surrounding him is the chaos of battle. The Corekai army has been pushed back by an overwhelming number of Corrupted. In the distance, he can see his friends, the other Tenkai Knights, battling a group of Sky Griffins.

As Bravenwolf prepares to enter Titan Mode, he spots Granox sneaking off.

If Bravenwolf should join up with the others to fight the Sky Griffins, head to page 64

If Bravenwolf should follow Granox, head to page 52

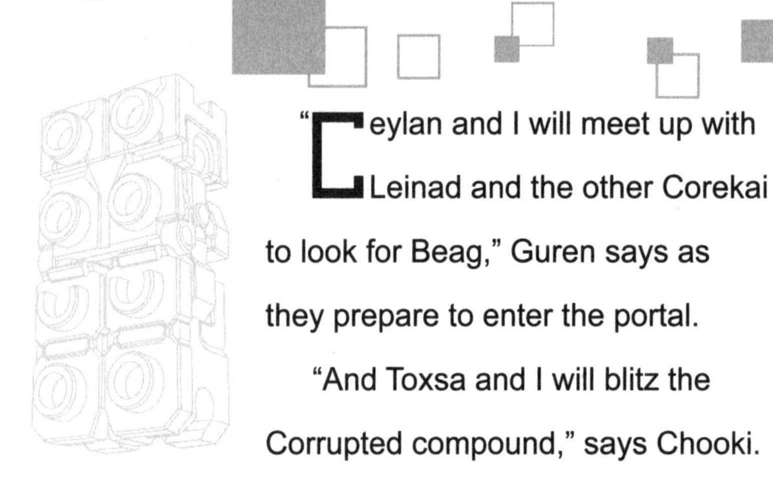

"Ceylan and I will meet up with Leinad and the other Corekai to look for Beag," Guren says as they prepare to enter the portal.

"And Toxsa and I will blitz the Corrupted compound," says Chooki.

Moments later, Guren and Ceylan are transported to the planet Quarton. As they arrive, the two boys shapeshift into the mighty Tenkai Knights Bravenwolf and Tributon.

A red-and-white Corekai soldier is waiting for them. "Bravenwolf! Tributon! It is an honor to have you join us in our search for Commander Beag," Leinad says. "There are several War Stallions guarding a small bunker just to the south of us. We believe that Beag is being held there."

"What if it's a trap?" Bravenwolf asks. "They

could be trying to lure us into an ambush."

"How about I go on ahead?" asks Tributon. "Bravenwolf, you can hold back and keep an eye out for an ambush."

Bravenwolf isn't sure that is the best idea.

If Tributon should check out the bunker on his own, head to page 23

If Tributon and Bravenwolf should stick together, head to page 27

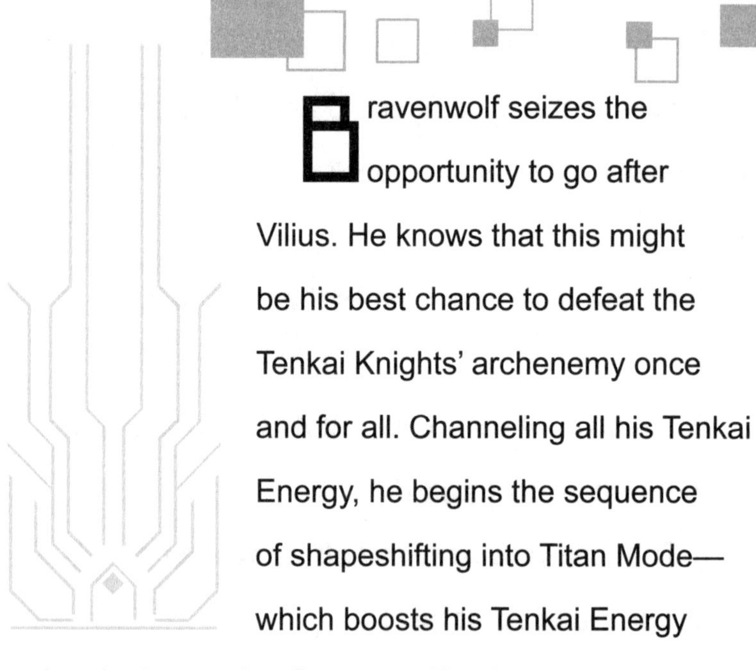

Bravenwolf seizes the opportunity to go after Vilius. He knows that this might be his best chance to defeat the Tenkai Knights' archenemy once and for all. Channeling all his Tenkai Energy, he begins the sequence of shapeshifting into Titan Mode—which boosts his Tenkai Energy levels, increasing Bravenwolf's size and strength. He'll need all the power he can muster to defeat such a strong foe.

TENKAI ENERGY AT 100 PERCENT. ACTIVATING TENKAI TITAN MODE.

Bravenwolf can sense the surge of Tenkai Energy in his power core as he shapeshifts into the massive Titan form of his Tenkai Knight.

Once the shapeshift is complete, Bravenwolf charges into battle. He holds his shield firmly as he raises his Tenkai Sword and prepares to engage his foe.

Vilius matches his attack by entering Titan Mode himself. Soon the two mighty warriors are standing face-to-face.

In the distance, Bravenwolf sees the Corrupted army overwhelming his friends. He knows that he's made an error in engaging Vilius on his own. He thought today would be the day that he defeated his greatest enemy—but he put his friends in danger. Now there is nothing he can do to save them.

The End

Valorn has a point. They still have a chance to defeat Shadius and rescue Beag before Vilius arrives.

"Okay, guys, follow me," Valorn says as he blasts Tenkai Energy from his spear at Shadius.

The other Knights follow behind him, firing attacks at the Corrupted as well.

Behind them, a Titan-size shadow spreads slowly across the battle. By the time they hear Vilius's laugh, it's too late.

The End

There are too many Corrupted soldiers closing in. Bravenwolf can't escape the oncoming attacks from the War Stallions.

"Bravenwolf!" Tributon calls out. "Free yourself and engage Titan Mode so we can fuse. Together we can defeat these guys."

Bravenwolf slams one of the stallions as hard as he can. The beast rears back, but others quickly take its place.

"I can't get away," Bravenwolf replies as everything slowly begins to go black.

The End

I can't wait around here forever, Guren thinks. *I have a bad feeling about this. I need to get to Quarton. The others can meet me there.*

He takes off from school and sprints toward Mr. White's shop. As he rounds the corner he sees Wakame, Toxsa's bossy older sister. As usual, she doesn't look happy.

"Hi, Wakame," Guren says as he slows down.

"Oh, Guren," she says. "Is my useless brother with you? I need his help at the restaurant, and I want to catch him before he gets in front of those video games of his."

"I haven't seen him since lunch," Guren replies.

"Hmmm," she says. "Well then, maybe you can help me."

“Uh. Um. You see,” Guren answers, “I’m in a bit of a, um, rush, and . . .”

Wakame gives him a glare that says that she isn’t going to take no for an answer.

If Guren should help Wakame, head to page 11

If Guren should continue on to Quarton, head to page 61

Guren sprints as fast as he can to Mr. White's shop. He had spent more time helping Wakame than he wanted to. The others were surely on Quarton already.

"What's going on?" Guren asks when he sees Mr. White's worried expression.

"Where have you been?" Mr. White says, ignoring Guren's question. "The others had to go without you. Beag's been captured. The others are doing their best to hold off Vilius and the Corrupted army, but I fear it's too late."

"No, I can still help them," Guren says as he approaches the portal. "I have to try."

Guren arrives on Quarton in the form of the Tenkai Knight Bravenwolf. All around him are defeated Corekai soldiers. In the distance, Vilius stands over the other Tenkai Knights, who appear to be beaten and exhausted.

"Looks like someone is a little late to the party," Vilius says with an evil laugh. "You're too late. I've defeated the Corekai and the other Tenkai Knights. The war is over, and you've lost."

Bravenwolf raises his sword and prepares to enter Titan Mode. Dozens of Corrupted soldiers and beasts amass around him. There is no way Bravenwolf will be able to defeat them all on his own.

Vilius laughs again in victory.

The End

Hoping that Granox might lead him to the place where the Corrupted are holding Beag, Bravenwolf breaks off and follows him. The horned gray soldier speeds down a long and winding path, heading far away from the battleground. Bravenwolf keeps just far enough back to avoid being spotted.

Granox suddenly stops and presses his shield against a rock—which then slides away, revealing a secret passage. The Corrupted soldier slips inside as the door begins to close around him.

Bravenwolf charges forward. Just as the secret door starts to vanish, he dives forward and jams his sword in the opening. The door struggles to close, but Bravenwolf summons his Tenkai Energy and forces it back open. Before him is a corridor filled with nothing but blackness.

Head to page 12

Guren transports to Quarton and shapeshifts into the Tenkai Knight Bravenwolf. Once there, he is struck by how empty and alone the planet feels. He walks for hours and sees no sign of the Corekai, or even Corrupted soldiers.

Then, in the distance, Bravenwolf sees the familiar sight of Tenkai Energy exploding in the air.

Climbing a rocky hill, he sees the other Tenkai Knights battling several War Stallions and an army of Corrupted soldiers.

The others must have transported together after I did, Bravenwolf thinks. *I should have waited for them. They look like they could use my help.*

Head to page 56

"About time you got here," Tributon calls out as Bravenwolf charges in beside his friends.

"Yeah, I thought maybe the cafeteria burger had taken its revenge on you," adds Valorn.

"How could it have?" Lydendor says. "You ate his burger before he even sat down. And then you tried to eat mine. I almost lost an arm fighting you off."

"Yeah, well—" Before Valorn can finish responding, a giant Sky Griffin swoops down and knocks Bravenwolf across the battlefield.

"*Aaaaaaah! Ummph!*" he yells as he skids to a stop.

Tributon fires his Tenkai Bow at the Corrupted beast, blasting it back far enough to give

Bravenwolf time to climb to his feet. "Look," he says, pointing to a group of Corrupted surrounding a multicolored Corekai soldier. "They're holding Beag over there."

Two more Sky Griffins rise up behind the first one, filling the sky with Corrupted beasts. Lydendor leaps forward and attacks with his Tenkai Chainsaber. The glowing yellow chain of Tenkai Energy crashes against the flying creature.

"Guys!" Bravenwolf calls out. "I think it's time for a little Robofusion."

Valorn lights up. "Yeah! It's Prodojet time!"

Head to page 74

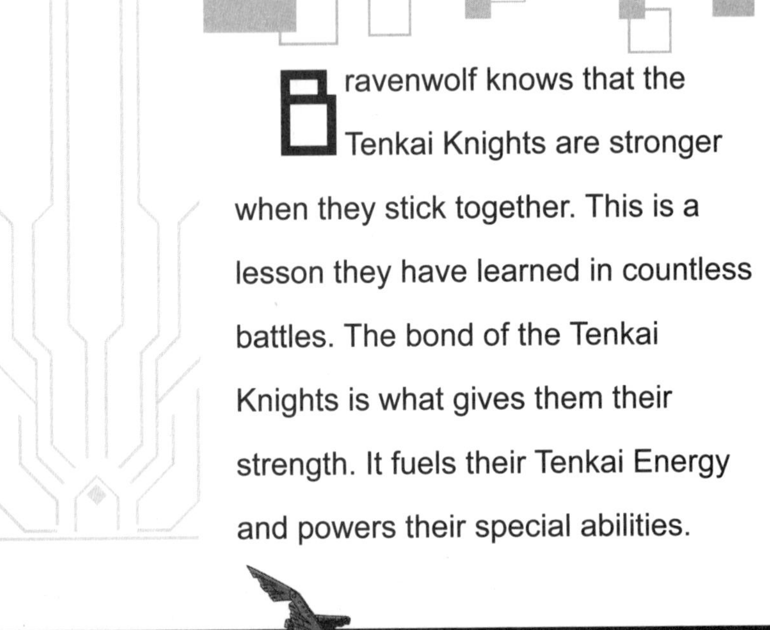

Bravenwolf knows that the Tenkai Knights are stronger when they stick together. This is a lesson they have learned in countless battles. The bond of the Tenkai Knights is what gives them their strength. It fuels their Tenkai Energy and powers their special abilities.

Bravenwolf charges through the oncoming Corrupted army, easily knocking soldiers aside as he makes his way toward his friends.

"Hold on, guys," he calls out as he slams a Corrupted soldier with his shield. "Bravenwolf is on his way!"

Together, the four Tenkai Knights—Bravenwolf, Tributon, Lydendor, and Valorn—stand together as one force. The War Stallions form an offensive

position before making their move. Bravenwolf uses his Tenkai Sword to smash one back as Valorn knocks another with his shield and follows up with a blast from his spear.

Unfortunately, Lydendor and Tributon aren't faring as well. The Corrupted War Stallions have them on the run.

If Bravenwolf and Valorn should stick with the War Stallions they're fighting, head to page 59

If the Tenkai Knights should enter Titan Mode, head to page 38

"Bravenwolf," Valorn calls out. "We need to enter Titan Mode to defeat these guys. Tributon and Lydendor need our help."

"Hold on a minute," Bravenwolf replies. "I think I've got this one." He attacks the War Stallion with his Tenkai Sword and smashes the beast to pieces. "See, I told you I had this one."

"That's not going to help our friends," says Valorn. "I can't even see them anymore through all those Corrupted soldiers."

"You're right, let's go."

Bravenwolf and Valorn plow through the War Stallions and Corrupted soldiers to find their friends—but they are nowhere to be seen.

"Vilius must have gotten them," Bravenwolf says. "This is all my fault. We should have stuck together as a team."

The End

Guren knows he should stay and help Wakame more, but there is no more time to waste. Leaving her behind, he runs as fast as he can to Mr. White's. When he gets there, the old man doesn't look happy.

"Guren, what took you so long?" he asks sternly. "The others have gone to Quarton without you."

"I'm sorry, Mr. White," he replies. "Something came up."

"You should get going. I'm sure they could use Bravenwolf's help."

Head to page 41

"I'll remember this the next time you're begging me for an extra side of fries!" Wakame yells as Guren runs off. He feels bad about not helping her, but he can't shake the feeling that something is happening on Quarton. As he sprints to Mr. White's store, he sees something out of the corner of his eye: a whole street appears to have become digital. It looks like Tenkai Energy from Quarton might be spilling over to Earth! Maybe that is what has Guren's senses so worked up.

If Guren should stop and explore the strange street, head to page 31

If Guren decides to continue on to Quarton, head to page 80

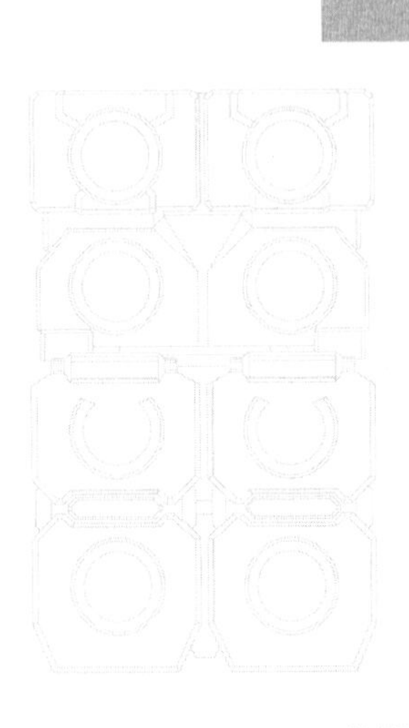

"A sneak attack is our best course of action," says Lydendor. "The Corekai should hide behind that rocky hill."

"And we'll wait behind this outcropping," Bravenwolf adds. "Once Vilius is close enough, we'll pop out, go all Titan, and take him out."

"Okay, team," says Lydendor. "Our best play here is a zone defense."

"A zone *what now*?" Valorn asks as Bravenwolf and Tributon nod in understanding.

"It's simple," Lydendor adds. "Everyone pick a spot and guard it. Don't let anyone draw you away from that spot. If we all stand our ground, Vilius won't be able to get past us. Then we'll have him where we want him."

The four Tenkai Knights take their positions and wait for Vilius and the Corrupted army to close in.

As the enemy approaches, Valorn spots Beag being held by a Corrupted soldier called Slyger. "I see Beag," he says to the others. "I'm going to go rescue him. This is just like in *Ninja Dungeon Hunter Three*. I'll sneak past those soldiers without them even seeing me."

"No, Valorn," Lydendor calls out. "It's a trap. If we take our focus off Vilius, we'll lose our advantage and we won't be able to save Beag . . . or ourselves."

"Fine," Valorn replies. "But it would have worked."

Head to page 21

Before Bravenwolf can do anything, a giant Sky Griffin swoops down and knocks Lydendor across the battlefield.

Tributon fires his Tenkai Bow at the Corrupted beast, but it dodges the attack. A second Sky Griffin flies up alongside the first, and together the creatures descend on the Tenkai Knight. Valorn rushes to defend his friend, but is scooped up by one of the beast's powerful claws.

Bravenwolf watches in horror as his friends are defeated.

The End

"I'm not hiding from a fight," Tributon says. "If Vilius wants to get us, then we should stand our ground and fight him."

With that, Tributon raises his bow and begins firing Tenkai Energy Arrows at the oncoming army.

"Well, it looks like we're fighting them head-on," Valorn says as he raises his spear and charges after Tributon.

Bravenwolf and Lydendor follow him.

Valorn spots Beag being held by a Corrupted soldier called Slyger. "I see Beag," he says to the others. "I'm going to go rescue him. This is just like in *Ninja Dungeon Hunter Three*. I'll sneak past those soldiers without them even seeing me."

"No, Valorn," Lydendor calls out. "It's a trap.

If we take our focus off Vilius, we'll lose our advantage and we won't be able to save Beag . . . or ourselves."

"Valorn might be right," says Bravenwolf. "This could be our only chance to rescue Beag. We have to try."

If you try to stop Vilius, head to page 21

If you let Vilius go and try to rescue Beag, head to page 32

"We're going to need all our strength to fight Vilius," Lydendor says. "Let's set up our defense now. There's no way we can let Vilius get to the end zone."

"Umm, what do you mean by 'end zone'?" Valorn asks. "I thought we were protecting the Corekai."

"They'll be here sooner than we thought," a blue-and-white soldier calls out. "Vilius and his army will arrive any minute now!"

Head to page 68

They decide that battling Vilius while they all are still strong is a wise move. The four Tenkai Knights take defensive positions around the Corekai encampment, knowing that the Corrupted are sneaky—they can come from anywhere.

After what seems like an eternity, a Corekai soldier calls out, “I see something! It’s the Corrupted army!”

Bravenwolf and the others quickly turn to see a massive army heading toward them. In the center is a familiar form: Vilius, the former Tenkai Knight who succumbed to evil and became the leader of the Corrupted.

"Let's go get him!" Valorn says as he raises his spear and shield.

"Hold up," Lydendor replies. "We can't just charge into battle. There are way more of them than there are of us. We need a plan."

"Agreed," adds Bravenwolf. "What if we plan a sneak attack? I don't think they've seen us yet."

If you think the Tenkai Knights should plan a sneak attack, head to page 62

If you think they should charge in and face Vilius, head to page 65

"I don't care if it's not the smartest move," Valorn says. "Beag is our friend. We have to rescue him now."

With that, the green Tenkai Knight leaves the others behind and charges off into the swarm of Corrupted soldiers that separate him from where Beag is being held.

"We have to go after him," Tributon says. "He'll get crushed if we let him go alone."

"Fine," Bravenwolf replies, powering down his Wolf Cannon. "But we need to—"

Bravenwolf is cut off as Vilius's Titan-size fist crashes into him, sending him skidding across the ground.

"The Bravenwolf I knew would never have let himself become distracted in battle," Vilius says as he presses his foot down on Bravenwolf's chest.

Bravenwolf struggles to stand up, but is pinned on the ground. Above him, Vilius raises his sword in victory.

The End

"We have to focus our attacks on Vilius," says Bravenwolf. "That's the only way we can save Beag."

Bravenwolf readies his special Tenkai Titan attack, the Wolf Cannon.

"He's right," Lydendor says as he readies his weapon, the mighty Chainsaber. "Vilius is our number one target."

Tributon isn't so sure about that plan. "I think I can get to Beag," he says. "You guys stay with Vilius."

"It's not safe to go on your own," says Bravenwolf.

If Bravenwolf decides to help his friend and follow after Tributon, head to page 30

If Bravenwolf lets Tributon go and continues with the attack, head to page 77

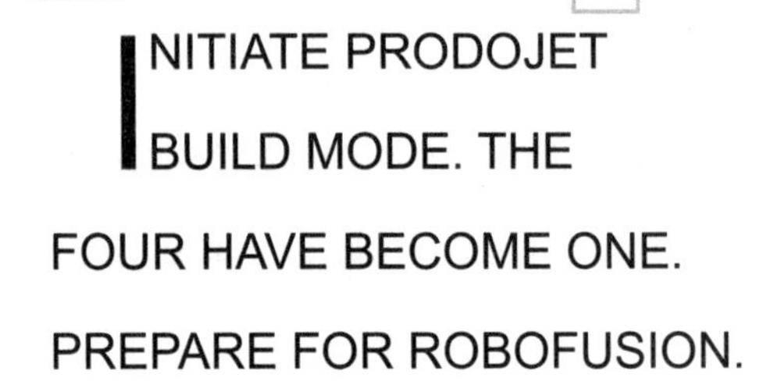

INITIATE PRODOJET BUILD MODE. THE FOUR HAVE BECOME ONE. PREPARE FOR ROBOFUSION.

They can feel an overwhelming surge in their Tenkai Energy as the four Tenkai Knights shapeshift together and form one mighty attack ship. The Prodojet has the red and blue coloring of Bravenwolf and Tributon, and is much more powerful than the four Tenkai Knights individually.

The Sky Griffins' attacks barely have any impact on the Prodojet.

"That's more like it," says Valorn. "This is like

having all the cheat codes."

"I'm not so sure," Bravenwolf adds. "Look!"

In the distance a familiar red-and-gray figure appears: Vilius. And he is in Titan Mode.

"I think our luck is about to run out," Lydendor says as they prepare to confront their ultimate foe.

The Tenkai Knights can hear Vilius's laughter as more Corrupted beasts descend on them. As they fight through the enemy, Vilius fades into the distance. There will be no battle today.

The Tenkai Knights easily defeat the Corrupted and free Beag, but not before Vilius gets away.

Tributon sprints off in the direction of where Beag is being held. Seconds later he vanishes from sight.

"Where did he go?" Bravenwolf calls to the others. "We have to find him."

"Let him go," Lydendor replies. "We have to fight Vilius. That's our only play."

Bravenwolf knows that Lydendor is right. Their only chance to rescue Beag and find Tributon is to defeat Vilius.

"Okay, but let's make this quick," Bravenwolf replies as he powers up his Tenkai Energy Wolf Cannon.

"You got it," says Valorn, and he and Lydendor prepare to engage their Titan Fusion—a transformation that combines their two Tenkai Knights into one massive warrior.

Bravenwolf and Vilius clash their mighty Titan weapons as Valorn and Lydendor attack from behind.

Vilius quickly disengages from the battle. "I may not have defeated all the Tenkai Knights today. But I have won a prize. Tributon is my prisoner now.

Soon I will have you all as my servants."

With that, he vanishes into the sky. On the ground in front of the three remaining Tenkai Knights is a dazed-looking Beag. They've rescued him as promised, but at what cost?

The End

Guren sprints as fast as he can to Mr. White's shop.

"What's going on?" Guren asks when he sees Mr. White's worried expression.

"Beag has been captured by Vilius," Mr. White says. "I don't know how much time there is for the Tenkai Knights to rescue him. Where are the others?"

"I don't know," Guren says. "I sensed that it was urgent, so I rushed here on my own."

"Hmmm," says Mr. White, stroking his beard. "I don't like the idea of you going on your own."

"What choice do we have?" Guren asks. "Beag's in trouble."

Head to page 53